HOW PLEASANT TO KNOW MR. LEAR!

Edward Lear's Selected Works
With an Introduction and Notes
BY

Myra Cohn Livingston

HOLIDAY HOUSE/NEW YORK

For Lloyd and Janine

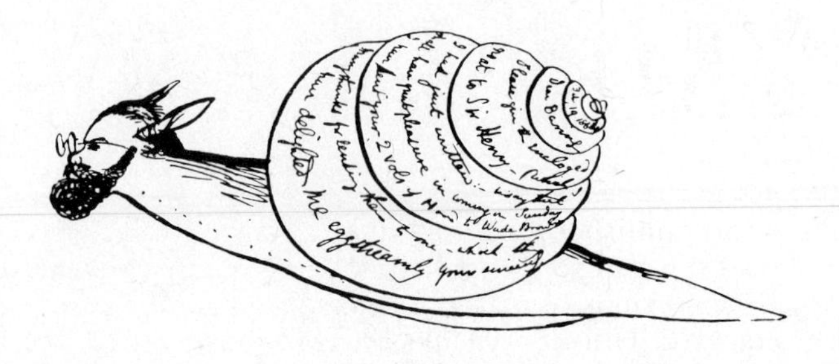

Printed in the United States of America
First Edition

Library of Congress Cataloging in Publication Data

Lear, Edward, 1812–1888.
How pleasant to know Mr. Lear!

Includes index.
Summary: A selection of nonsense verse, with the author's illustrations, by the great nineteenth-century English humorist. Includes biographical introduction and notes.
1. Nonsense-verses, English. [1. Nonsense verses.
2. Humorous poetry. 3. English poetry. 4. Lear,
Edward, 1812–1888] I. Livingston, Myra Cohn. II. Title.
PR4879.L2A6 1982 821'.8 82-80822
ISBN 0-8234-0462-5 AACR2

Acknowledgments

The editor and publisher wish to thank Osborne Clarke as Administrators of Constance S. Ester Cipelletti Lady Strachey deceased for permission to use portions of material reproduced in this book; Houghton Library, Harvard University, Department of Printing and Graphic Arts, and John Murray, Ltd. for permission to reprint "Chimnies and Wings," "The Dish Tree," "Herons and Sweeps," "Puddings and beams," and "Wafers and Bears" from *Teapots and Quails*, eds. Angus Davidson and Philip Hofer (1953), and Houghton Library for making reproductions of these five selections available for reprinting in this book; Department of Special Collections, University Research Library, University of California at Los Angeles, for reproducing thirty-one drawings from original source material for this book; Justin Schiller for his kindness in providing material from which twenty-three of Lear's drawings could be reproduced for this book; Dodd, Mead & Co., Inc. for permission to reproduce textual material from *The Complete Nonsense Book* by Edward Lear, edited by Lady Strachey, with an introduction by the Earl of Cromer (1958).

The editor wishes to thank Hilda Boehm, Librarian in Special Collections, University Research Library, University of California at Los Angeles, for her help in making available the nonsense books of Edward Lear; to Vivien Noakes for her book, *Edward Lear, The Life of a Wanderer* (Houghton Mifflin, 1969), the only source for diary material referred to in the notes. Other bibliographic material includes *A Book of Nonsense* (Routledge, Warne and Routledge, second and enlarged edition, 1861); *Nonsense Songs, Stories, Botany, and Alphabets* (Robert John Bush, 1871); *More Nonsense, Pictures, Rhymes, Botany, etc.* (Robert John Bush, 1872); and *Laughable Lyrics: A Fourth Book of Nonsense Poems, Songs, Botany, Music &c.* (Robert John Bush, 1877); *Journals of a Landscape Painter in Albania, &c.* (Richard Bentley, 1851); *Journals of a Landscape Painter in Southern Calabria, &c.* (Richard Bentley, 1852); all of the aforementioned titles by Edward

Lear; *Queery Leary Nonsense*, ed. Lady Strachey (Mills & Boon, 1911); *Letters of Edward Lear*, ed. Lady Strachey (Duffield & Co., 1911); *Later Letters of Edward Lear*, ed. Lady Strachey (Duffield & Co., 1911); *Edward Lear's Journals: A Selection*, ed. H. Van Thal (Arthur Barker, 1952); *The Poetry of Nonsense*, Emile Cammaerts (E. P. Dutton, 1926); *A Handful of Authors*, G. K. Chesterton (Sheed & Ward, 1953); *The Field of Nonsense*, Elizabeth Sewell (Chatto & Windus, 1952); *Teapots and Quails*, eds. Angus Davidson and Philip Hofer (Harvard University Press, 1954).

Contents

Introduction

How pleasant to know Edward Lear, the "crazy old Englishman" whose beard looked like a wig, who was spherical in shape, ill-tempered and queer to some, yet pleasant to others and who purchased chocolate shrimps! And what fun to imagine how his poem must have pleased the Bevan children whom he met at the time he wrote it, just one hundred years ago.

A century later we can still delight in this poem, for it tells us something of how Edward Lear looked at himself. He was sixty-seven years old at the time, a man who had spent his life wishing to be a great landscape artist, or, as he himself wrote, "nartist" who drew "pigchers" and "vorx of hart." Yet he is remembered and loved most for the nonsense he wrote and sketches he drew to make children happy. Such a person arouses our curiosity. There is certainly more to Lear than he suggests in his autobiographical poem.

"If I write nonsense," he once told a friend, "I am pervaded with smiles." Lear needed the nonsense and the smiles, for his life was never an easy one. It is astounding that he was able to turn all the difficult circumstances of his childhood and adult life, the "heaps of small botherations," into limericks, story poems and humorous drawings that brought his readers such joy. This is perhaps the secret of Edward Lear; he was so sensitive to what made him unhappy and lonely that he wished to give others laughter, to have them think of him as "3 parts crazy—& wholly affectionate."

From what is known of his early life, Edward Lear was always an affectionate, although lonely, boy. Born in 1812, he was the twentieth child in a family of twenty-one. His father lost his money when Lear was three years old; he rarely saw his parents for his mother, overburdened with her large family, put him in the care of older sisters. His father seemed to have had no time for him. At seven he developed moods of depression which he named "The Morbids," but even before this he had suffered his first attack of epilepsy. Epilepsy was then a dreaded word, something shameful and secret. There was no known cure and these seizures, which he called "The Demons," persisted throughout his life. In addition, he was subject to asthma and rheumatism. (Lear described them as "assma roomtizim.") His health was a never-ending source of trouble to him.

Raised by an older sister, Ann, he knew, too, the difficulties of poverty. At sixteen he began to earn his own living by drawing parrots and became so successful that he was sought by naturalists and zoologists to draw other birds and animals as well. Many of his drawings were published, and he himself published a book on parrots.

At twenty he was invited by Lord Stanley, heir to the Earl of Derby, to stay at Knowsley, the Earl's estate, to make drawings of his private menagerie. It was here that he began to write limericks and draw amusing sketches for the entertainment of the children who lived in and visited the large country house. Lear worked on and off at Knowsley for five years, but it was difficult work because his eyes, never too good, had begun to trouble him.

Lear's temperament was not suited to the boredom of country-house society. There is "nothing I long for half so much as to giggle heartily," he told a friend, "and to hop on one leg down the great gallery—but I dare not." The "moneytryingintoget smoky-dark Londonlife" did not agree with his health either. He left England for Italy when he was twenty-five, hoping to improve his health and to study landscape painting.

Although he returned to England for occasional visits, Lear spent the rest of his life wandering from country to country, always hoping to become a great "landskip" painter. But his work was not as popular as that of other artists of his day. The success he achieved during his lifetime was mainly for his nonsense verses and sketches, published in five books from the time he was thirty-four to sixty-five years old.

Lear traveled to many a "fifflefaddle poodly-pumpkin place" by himself or with friends. His diaries and letters abound with "ozbervations"—his joys at discovering the "wonder of foliage" and the "pomskizillious and gromphibberous" coast scenery of Italy, Albania, the Greek islands and many other countries. He would write of the "grumpy roargroanery of camels" in Egypt or when, during a cold winter, frozen waterpipes began to thaw, he told a friend of the "horrible borrible squashfibolious meligoposhquilious sounds . . . like 50,000 whales in hysterics." He wrote seven books about his own travels, kept a diary and wrote letters continually to his friends. It is in the letters and diaries that the richness of his word invention and unusual spelling is recorded for us to enjoy.

He loved to play with words. The sound of a rolling river was "meloobious," and he described a kind of a melody as "mumbian." Leaving for England, he packed "furibundiously." "Scroobious," a word he used frequently, was closely related to "dubious doubtfulness." "Bundy," "Toosday" and "Weddlesday" were days of the week; and "Joon" was two months before "Orgst," just before "Ortum." Indeed, he invented hundreds of such words, some of which appear in his nonsense verse. Writing of an imaginary trip to the moon, he created "Jizzdoddle" rocks, a "Rumbytumby" ravine, a "blompopp" tree and "Ambelboff" pies.

Lear was overly conscious of his physical appearance. He spoke very often of his "well-developed nose." His writing tended to exaggerate this as well as his bushy beard, long legs, "tenda" feet, rotund body and nearsightedness. It is doubtful that he was as "hideous" as his poem would have us believe, for children were always delighted to be with him. It is certain that he used these features for the purpose of amusing his listeners and readers. "The Dong with the Luminous Nose" and many of his limerick people are conscious of their "remarkably big" or odd noses. It is Aunt Jobiska who says that no harm will come to "The Pobble Who Has No Toes"—"if his nose is warm."

Lear's own beard inspired him to write about others who had beards, whiskers and strange hairdos. He invented persons whose appearance was as odd as he fancied his own to be, often in garments as unusual as his own loose-fitting clothing. If he could "not abide ginger beer" but enjoyed "chocolate shrimps," he created others who ate and drank peculiar mixtures. His own "runcible" hat is shown in many guises, whether it belongs to the Quangle Wangle or the Scroobious Snake or adorns the heads of his limerick people.

The story poems that he set to music are evidence that he was "one of the singers" who enjoyed playing the piano and singing although he had no formal musical training. He wrote about the singers as well as "the dumbs" that he knew or imagined. And what fun it is to meet Lear's imaginary creatures, not only in the poems that bear their names, but creeping into other verses. The Pobble and the Dong flock to "The Quangle Wangle's Hat" along with other birds. The chorus of "The Jumblies" is heard in the poem about "The Dong with the Luminous Nose." The Jumblies visit the hills of the Chankly Bore where Daughter Dell of "The Pelican Chorus" lives, as well as the Dong. "The Duck and the Kangaroo" contemplate a trip to the Jelly Bo Lee, a place that "The Scroobious Pip" also sees.

Lear's love for birds of all kinds appears in almost all of his story poems, whether they be owls, ducks, pelicans, sparrows or imaginary creatures such as the Fimble Fowl with the Corkscrew leg. Lear once described himself as "blind as an owl, dark as a raven, and gaudy as a parrot," and he pictured many people as birds, and personified birds as people.

Lear laughed a great deal, but he also admitted that he wept—giving to his work a quality that cannot be dismissed as mere silliness or pointless nonsense. Certainly one of the best known and loved of his story poems is "The Owl and the Pussy-Cat." It is here that many of the themes and symbols meaningful to him appear. His affection for birds and devotion to cats, who might seem to be natural enemies in real life, become the happy pair who sail off on a voyage to distant places. Lear's love of travel, his feeling for music, his pleasure in eating, his love of animals, his determination to be cheerful in spite of all obstacles result in a happy ending with dancing upon a distant shore.

We can read "The Owl and the Pussy-Cat" as a nonsense poem about an unlikely happening, but we can also be aware that in a sense it is a fantasy of a life Edward Lear wished for himself. Although we know from his letters and diaries that he thought about it on several occasions, he never married. His constant worry about "plenty of money," his longing to be an "elegant" creature who could charm a lady, buy her a ring and live happily ever after are real feelings that we may find in this poem.

Lear's search for love is re-echoed in much of his work, but particularly in "The Courtship of the Yonghy-Bonghy-Bò." Here is a creature with an absurd name, little in the way of worldly goods, rejected by the Lady Jingly. Initially, it may appear to be a funny poem with nonsensical names, but one has only to know something of Lear's life—of how he burst into tears when singing and playing this on the piano—to feel its underlying sadness.

Yet Lear wished, above all, to "make little folks merry" and never lost touch with the child in himself. Writing in his diary when he was seventy-one years old, he noted that "Life today is happier than this child deserves. . . ." It is this ability to remember childhood and to preserve the limitless possibilities of a child's humor and imagination that still delight us in his work after so many years.

However we read Edward Lear, with laughter or with an understanding of his underlying sadness, we will find in his work a very human man who somehow managed to let the joys outweigh the sorrows throughout "the days of his pilgrimage."

MYRA COHN LIVINGSTON
August, 1979

How Pleasant to Know Mr. Lear!

How pleasant to know Mr. Lear!
  Who has written such volumes of stuff!
Some think him ill-tempered and queer,
  But a few think him pleasant enough.

His mind is concrete and fastidious,
  His nose is remarkably big;
His visage is more or less hideous,
  His beard it resembles a wig.

He has ears, and two eyes, and ten fingers,
  Leastways if you reckon two thumbs,
Long ago he was one of the singers,
  But now he is one of the dumbs.

He sits in a beautiful parlour,
  With hundreds of books on the wall;
He drinks a great deal of Marsala,
  But never gets tipsy at all.

He has many friends, laymen and clerical;
  Old Foss is the name of his cat;
His body is perfectly spherical,
  He weareth a runcible hat.

When he walks in a waterproof white,
  The children run after him so!
Calling out, "He's come out in his night-
  Gown, that crazy old Englishman, oh!"

He weeps by the side of the ocean,
He weeps on the top of the hill;
He purchases pancakes and lotion,
And chocolate shrimps from the mill.

He reads but he cannot speak Spanish,
He cannot abide ginger beer;
Ere the days of his pilgrimage vanish,
How pleasant to know Mr. Lear!

1/ *"Ill-Tempered and Queer"*

"If I can't sleep," Lear once wrote to a friend, "my whole system seems to turn into pins, cayenne-pepper, & vinegar and I suffer hideously. . . . Then what the devil can I do? Buy a baboon & a parrot & let them rush about the room?" Lear often recorded times when he found himself in a "crooked frame of mind" or became "mentally decompoged."

Cold weather, bumpy railway journeys, noisy neighbors, "vulgarry people" and "beastly aristocratic idiots" were among the annoyances that could bring out his "bilious and skrogfrodious temperament." During his travels he encountered others whose behavior seemed erratic: a woman in Greece who tore out her hair, Albanians who subsisted on strange roots, and a "splitmecrackle crashmecriggle . . . howling belowstairs" singer in Rome. If he felt himself "unstable and ass-like" or behaving like a "fidgety kangaroo," he could also compare hotel guests to "Octopeds and Reptiles" who were "howly-gabbling" about the halls and stairs.

The irritations of life, the "ojous" or unpleasant times when life became "werry werry pongdomphious" abounded. But Lear was always able to turn these fits of temper into amusements for his readers.

There was an old person of Crowle,
Who lived in the nest of an owl;
When they screamed in the nest,
He screamed out with the rest,
That depressing old person of Crowle.

There was an old person of Sestri,
Who sate himself down in the vestry;
When they said "You are wrong!"
He merely said "Bong!"
That repulsive old person of Sestri.

There was an Old Person of Bangor,
Whose face was distorted with anger,
He tore off his boots,
And subsisted on roots,
That borascible person of Bangor.

There was an old person of Bromley,
Whose ways were not cheerful or comely;
He sate in the dust,
Eating spiders and crust,
That unpleasing old person of Bromley.

There was an old person of Down,
Whose face was adorned with a frown;
When he opened the door,
For one minute or more,
He alarmed all the people of Down.

There was an old man of Ibreem,
Who suddenly threaten'd to scream:
But they said, "If you do,
We will thump you quite blue,
You disgusting old man of Ibreem!"

There was an old person of Newry,
Whose manners were tinctured with fury;
He tore all the rugs,
And broke all the jugs
Within twenty miles' distance of Newry.

There was an Old Man of Peru,
Who never knew what he should do;
So he tore off his hair,
And behaved like a bear,
That intrinsic Old Man of Peru.

There was an Old Person of Anerley,
Whose conduct was strange and unmannerly;
    He rushed down the Strand,
    With a Pig in each hand,
But returned in the evening to Anerley.

There was an old person of Bude,
Whose deportment was vicious and crude;
    He wore a large ruff
    Of pale straw-colored stuff,
Which perplexed all the people of Bude.

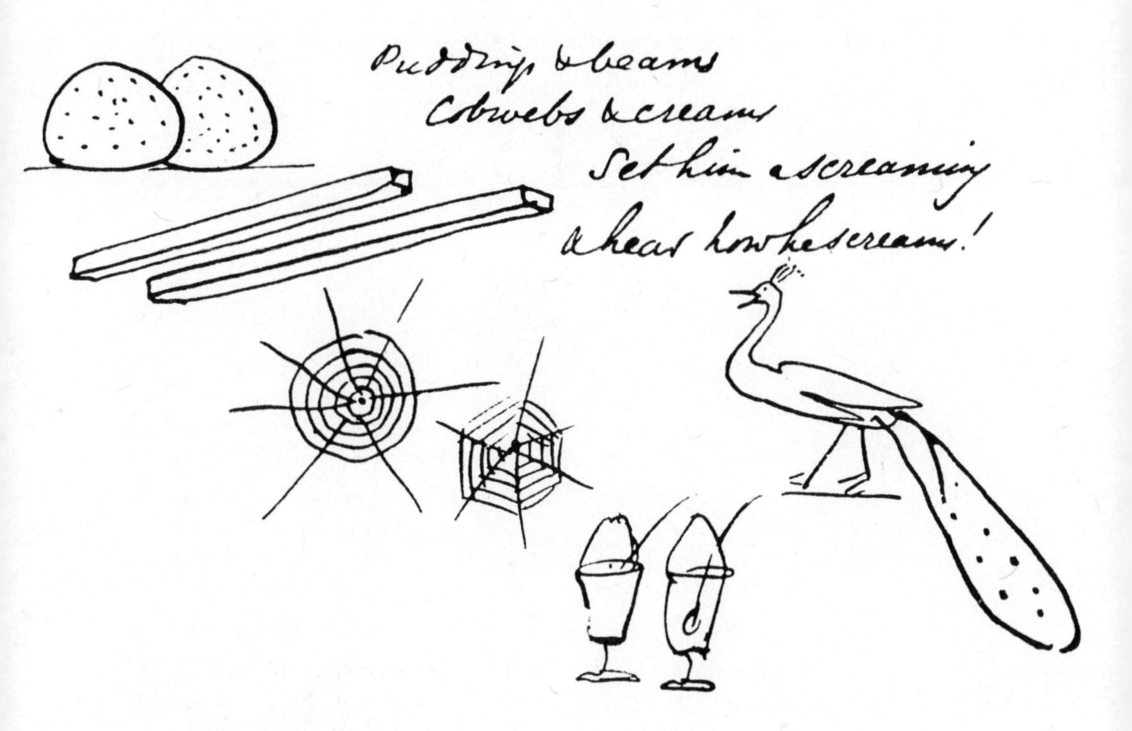

Puddings and beams,
Cobwebs and creams,
Set him a screaming
and hear how he screams!

2/ *"His Nose Is Remarkably Big"*

When he was twenty, Lear drew a self-portrait that he described in his usual nonsensical vein: "both my knees are fractured from being run over which has made them peculiarly crooked— . . . my neck is singularly long—a most elephantine nose—& a disposition to tumble here & there—owing to being half-blind. . . ."

Lear's nose obsessed him more than any other facial feature. He gave many of his limerick characters most unusual noses—noses with tassels at the end, noses so long they could be used for resting things on, or strange noses that made others laugh. "The cold is so great," he wrote to a friend from England, "that my nose is frizz so hard that I use it as a paper cutter."

"The Dong with the Luminous Nose" is one of Lear's most serious poems, written at a time in life when he had probably given up hope of finding his "Jumbly girl." Yet it was characteristic of Lear that he should utilize the very feature of his face he disliked most as a symbol of hope. Through his art, he would transform misfortune into a "lonely spark" of optimism, never ceasing in the search of his lost love, or in "piercing the coal-black night" for a resolution to his loneliness.

"His Nose Is Remarkably Big"

There was an old person of Cassel,
Whose nose finished off in a tassel;
    But they call'd out, "Oh well!—
    Don't it look like a bell!"
Which perplexed that old person of Cassel.

There is a young lady, whose nose,
Continually prospers and grows;
    When it grew out of sight,
    She exclaimed in a fright,
"Oh! Farewell to the end of my nose!"

There was an Old Man, on whose nose,
Most birds of the air could repose;
But they all flew away,
At the closing of day,
Which relieved that Old Man and his nose.

There was an Old Man with a nose,
Who said, "If you choose to suppose,
That my nose is too long,
You are certainly wrong!"
That remarkable Man with a nose.

There was an old man of Dunrose;
A parrot seized hold of his nose.
    When he grew melancholy,
    They said, "His name's Polly,"
Which soothed that old man of Dunrose.

There was a Young Lady whose nose,
Was so long that it reached to her toes;
    So she hired an Old Lady,
    Whose conduct was steady,
To carry that wonderful nose.

There was an old man of West Dumpet,
Who possessed a large nose like a trumpet;
When he blew it aloud,
It astonished the crowd,
And was heard through the whole of West Dumpet.

There was an Old Person of Tring,
Who embellished his nose with a ring;
He gazed at the moon,
Every evening in June,
That ecstatic Old Person of Tring.

"His Nose Is Remarkably Big"

There was an old man in a barge,
Whose nose was exceedingly large;
    But in fishing by night,
    It supported a light,
Which helped that old man in a barge.

The Dong with a Luminous Nose

When awful darkness and silence reign
Over the great Gromboolian plain,
  Through the long, long wintry nights;—
When the angry breakers roar
As they beat on the rocky shore;—
  When Storm-clouds brood on the towering heights
Of the Hills of the Chankly Bore:—

Then, through the vast and gloomy dark,
There moves what seems a fiery spark,
  A lonely spark with silvery rays
  Piercing the coal-black night,—
  A Meteor strange and bright:—
Hither and thither the vision strays,
  A single lurid light.

Slowly it wanders,—pauses,—creeps,—
Anon it sparkles,—flashes and leaps;
And ever as onward it gleaming goes
A light on the Bong-tree stems it throws.
And those who watch at that midnight hour
From Hall or Terrace, or lofty Tower,
Cry, as the wild light passes along,—
"The Dong!—the Dong!
The wandering Dong through the forest goes!
The Dong! the Dong!
The Dong with a luminous Nose!"

Long years ago
The Dong was happy and gay,
Till he fell in love with a Jumbly Girl
Who came to those shores one day,
For the Jumblies came in a sieve, they did,—
Landing at eve near the Zemmery Fidd
Where the Oblong Oysters grow,
And the rocks are smooth and gray.
And all the woods and the valleys rang
With the Chorus they daily and nightly sang,—
"Far and few, far and few,
Are the lands where the Jumblies live;
Their heads are green, and their hands are blue
And they went to sea in a sieve."

Happily, happily passed those days!
While the cheerful Jumblies staid;
They danced in circlets all night long,
To the plaintive pipe of the lively Dong,
In moonlight, shine, or shade.
For day and night he was always there
By the side of the Jumbly Girl so fair,
With her sky-blue hands, and her sea-green hair.
Till the morning came of that hateful day
When the Jumblies sailed in their sieve away,
And the Dong was left on the cruel shore

Gazing—gazing for evermore,—
Ever keeping his weary eyes on
That pea-green sail on the far horizon,—
Singing the Jumbly Chorus still
As he sate all day on the grassy hill,—
"Far and few, far and few,
Are the lands where the Jumblies live;
Their heads are green, and their hands are blue,
And they went to sea in a sieve."

But when the sun was low in the West,
The Dong arose and said;—
—"What little sense I once possessed
Has quite gone out of my head!"—
And since that day he wanders still
By lake and forest, marsh and hill,
Singing—"O somewhere, in valley or plain
Might I find my Jumbly Girl again!
For ever I'll seek by lake and shore
Till I find my Jumbly Girl once more!"

Playing a pipe with silvery squeaks,
Since then his Jumbly Girl he seeks,
And because by night he could not see,
He gathered the bark of the Twangum Tree
On the flowery plain that grows.
And he wove him a wondrous Nose,—
A Nose as strange as a Nose could be!
Of vast proportions and painted red,
And tied with cords to the back of his head.
—In a hollow rounded space it ended
With a luminous Lamp within suspended,
All fenced about
With a bandage stout
To prevent the wind from blowing it out;—
And with holes all round to send the light,
In gleaming rays on the dismal night.

And now each night, and all night long,
Over those plains still roams the Dong;
And above the wail of the Chimp and Snipe
You may hear the squeak of his plaintive pipe
While ever he seeks, but seeks in vain
To meet with his Jumbly Girl again;
Lonely and wild—all night he goes,—
The Dong with a luminous Nose!
And all who watch at the midnight hour,
From Hall or Terrace, or lofty Tower,
Cry, as they trace the Meteor bright,
Moving along through the dreary night,—
    "This is the hour when forth he goes,
    The Dong with a luminous Nose!
    Yonder—over the plain he goes;
        He goes!
        He goes;
    The Dong with a luminous Nose!"

There was an Old Man of the South,
Who had an immoderate mouth;
 But in swallowing a dish,
 That was quite full of fish,
He was choked, that Old Man of the South.

There was an old man of Dumblane,
Who greatly resembled a crane;
 But they said,—"Is it wrong,
 Since your legs are so long,
To request you won't stay in Dumblane?"

There was an old person of Nice,
Whose associates were usually Geese.
They walked out together,
In all sorts of weather.
That affable person of Nice!

There was a Young Lady whose eyes,
Were unique as to color and size;
When she opened them wide,
People all turned aside,
And started away in surprise.

There was an Old Man of the West,
Who never could get any rest;
So they set him to spin,
On his nose and his chin,
Which cured that Old Man of the West.

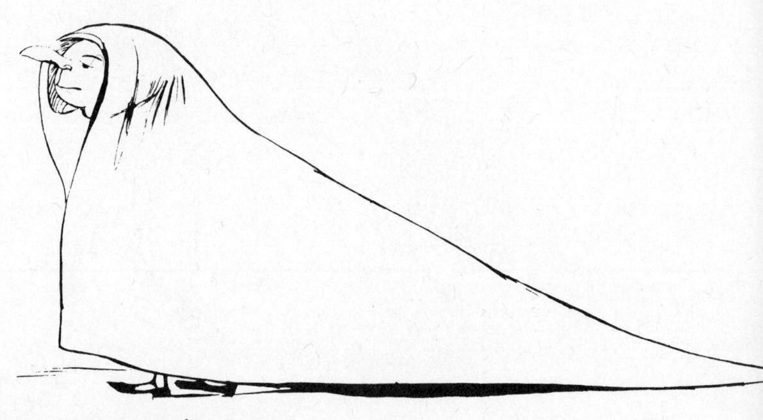

There was a young person in green,
Who seldom was fit to be seen;
She wore a long shawl,
Over bonnet and all,
Which enveloped that person in green.

There was an Old Man who said, "Hush!
I perceive a young bird in this bush!"
When they said—"Is it small?"
He replied—"Not at all!
It is four times as big as the bush!"

There was an old person of Skye,
Who waltz'd with a Bluebottle fly:
They buzz'd a sweet tune,
To the light of the moon,
And entranced all the people of Skye.

The Umbrageous Umbrella-maker,
whose Face nobody ever saw, because it was
always covered by his Umbrella.

Wafers and Bears,
Ladders and Squares,
Set him a staring
and see how he stares!

4/ *"His Beard It Resembles a Wig"*

Often, journeying by boat, Lear would grow a beard only to shave it off when he returned home. During a tiresome ten-week voyage in 1854 he grew a bushy beard which he kept ever afterwards. It made him look, he wrote to a friend, "half way between Socrates and Sir John Falstaff."

From Malta, in 1862, Lear drew a sketch of himself with a huge halo of hair noting that it had taken "a violent excess of growth of late." At sixty-seven he wrote that his hair was "falling off, and I rejoice to think that the misery of hair cutting will soon cease." At Corfu he recalled an incident when he was painting, "having a full palate & brushes in hand" and looked out of the window as a parade of soldiers marched past. "Col. Bruce saw me and saluted; & not liking to make a formillier nod in presence of the hole harmy, I put up my hand to salute,—& thereby transfered all my colours into my hair & whiskers—which I must now wash in Turpentine or shave off."

Hair styles always captivated his imagination. His journals record "the long matted hair and moustache" of the men of Draghiadhes. Crossing the desert by camel from Cairo to Gaza, he wrote in his diary that it was "*not pleasant*" to find "beetles in your hair." This is reflected in the man from Blackheath who wears a wreath of "lobsters and spice, pickled onions and mice."

It was perfectly natural in Lear's nonsense world for a raven to wear a white wig or a jay to do up her hair in roses.

There was an Old Man with a beard,
Who said, "It is just as I feared!—
Two Owls and a Hen,
Four Larks and a Wren,
Have all built their nests in my beard!"

There was an old person of Brigg,
Who purchased no end of a wig;
So that only his nose,
And the end of his toes,
Could be seen when he walked about Brigg.

There was an old man in a tree,
Whose whiskers were lovely to see;
　　But the birds of the air,
　　Pluck'd them perfectly bare,
To make themselves nests in that tree.

There was an old man of Blackheath,
Whose head was adorned with a wreath,
　　Of lobsters and spice,
　　Pickled onions and mice,
That uncommon old man of Blackheath.

There was an old person of Dutton,
Whose head was so small as a button:
So to make it look big,
He purchased a wig,
And rapidly rushed about Dutton.

There was a young lady of Firle,
Whose hair was addicted to curl;
It curled up a tree,
And all over the sea,
That expansive young lady of Firle.

There was an old man of Messina,
Whose daughter was named Opsibeena;
    She wore a small wig,
    And rode out on a pig,
To the perfect delight of Messina.

There was an Old Man with a beard,
Who sat on a horse when he reared;
    But they said, "Never mind!
    You will fall off behind,
You propitious Old Man with a beard!"

The Judicious Jubilant Jay,
who did up her Back Hair every morning with a Wreath of Roses
Three feathers, and a Gold Pin.

The Rural Runcible Raven,
who wore a White Wig and flew away
with the Carpet Broom.

5/ *"One of the Singers"*

Although Lear had no formal musical training and could not read music, he delighted in playing the piano and singing for special friends. He set a number of his story poems to music as well as some of the work of Alfred, Lord Tennyson. "Tears, Idle Tears" was one of Lear's favorites. This poem and his own "The Courtship of the Yonghy-Bonghy-Bò" often would make him burst into tears.

A popular after-dinner entertainer, he performed with alternate humor and pathos, taking into account the company and the mood. Writing to a friend from Surrey in September, 1860, he explained his life at the Oatlands Park Hotel. "At 9. I go to my room, much to the disgust of the community who having found out that I am musical, sent up a deputation 2 nights ago to ask me to come down to them—but I remained where I was." Three years later he wrote to the same friend from Corfu, telling of his happy life. "I am collapsing with laughter and must go and bounce chords on the Piano."

Music, singing and dancing appear in many of his verses and drawings. Lyres, harps, bells, flutes, fiddles and other instruments are played in most unusual ways, by both people and animals. "The Pelican Chorus" is one example of a song that the pelicans "nightly snort," set to music by Lear.

Guittara Pensilis

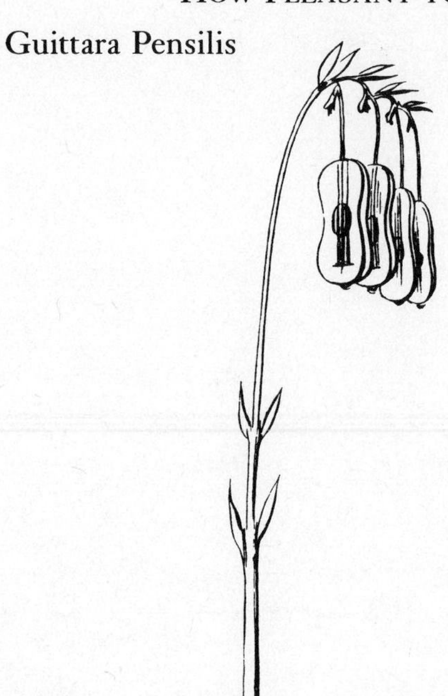

There was a Young Lady whose chin,
Resembled the point of a pin;
So she had it made sharp,
And purchased a harp,
And played several tunes with her chin.

"One of the Singers"

There was an old man in a Marsh,
Whose manners were futile and harsh;
He sate on a log,
And sang songs to a frog,
That instructive old man in a Marsh.

There was an Old Man of the Isles,
Whose face was pervaded with smiles:
He sung high dum diddle,
And played on the fiddle,
That amiable Man of the Isles.

There was a Young Lady of Bute,
Who played on a silver-gilt flute;
She played several jigs,
To her uncle's white pigs,
That amusing Young Lady of Bute.

There was an Old Man with a gong,
Who bumped at it all the day long;
But they called out, "O law!
You're a horrid old bore!"
So they smashed that Old Man with a gong.

There was a Young Lady of Welling,
Whose praise all the world was a telling;
    She played on the harp,
    And caught several carp,
That accomplished Young Lady of Welling.

There was a young Lady of Tyre,
Who swept the loud chords of a lyre;
    At the sound of each sweep,
    She enraptured the deep,
And enchanted the city of Tyre.

There was an old person of Jodd,
Whose ways were perplexing and odd;
She purchased a whistle,
And sate on a thistle,
And squeaked to the people of Jodd.

There was an old person of Filey,
Of whom his acquaintance spoke highly;
He danced perfectly well,
To the sound of a bell,
And delighted the people of Filey.

There was an Old Man with a flute,
A sarpint ran into his boot;
    But he played day and night,
    Till the sarpint took flight,
And avoided that man with a flute.

The Melodious Meritorious Mouse,
who played a merry minuet on the
Piano-forte.

The Tumultuous Tom-tommy Tortoise, who beat a Drum all day long in the middle of the wilderness.

The Worrying Whizzing Wasp, who stood on a Table, and played sweetly on a Flute with a Morning Cap.

"One of the Singers"

Chimnies and Wings,
Sailors and Rings,
Set him a singing
and hark how he sings!

THE PELICANS.
CANTO.
PIANO.
King and Queen of the Peli-cans we, No other birds so grand we see!
None but we have feet like fins with love-ly lea-the-ry throats and chins,
Coro—piu sostenuto.
Ploff-skin, Pluff-skin, Pe-li-can Jee! we think no birds so hap-py as we!
Plump-skin, Ploff-skin, Pe-li-can Jill! We think so then, and we thought so still!

The Pelican Chorus

King and Queen of the Pelicans we;
No other Birds so grand we see!
None but we have feet like fins!
With lovely leathery throats and chins!
    Ploffskin, Pluffskin, Pelican jee!
    We think no Birds so happy as we!
    Plumpskin, Ploshkin, Pelican jill!
    We think so then, and we thought so still!
We live on the Nile. The Nile we love.
By night we sleep on the cliffs above;
By day we fish, and at eve we stand
On long bare islands of yellow sand.
And when the sun sinks slowly down
And the great rock walls grow dark and brown,
Where the purple river rolls fast and dim
And the Ivory Ibis starlike skim,
Wing to wing we dance around,—
Stamping our feet with a flumpy sound,—
Opening our mouths as Pelicans ought,
And this is the song we nightly snort;—
    Ploffskin, Pluffskin, Pelican jee,—
    We think no Birds so happy as we!
    Plumpskin, Ploshkin, Pelican jill,—
    We think so then, and we thought so still.

Last year came out our Daughter, Dell;
And all the Birds received her well.
To do her honor, a feast we made
For every bird that can swim or wade.
Herons and Gulls, and Cormorants black,
Cranes, and Flamingoes with scarlet back,
Plovers and Storks, and Geese in clouds,
Swans and Dilberry Ducks in crowds.
Thousands of Birds in wondrous flight!
They ate and drank and danced all night,
And echoing back from the rocks you heard
Multitude-echoes from Bird and Bird,—
    Ploffskin, Pluffskin, Pelican jee,
    We think no Birds so happy as we!
    Plumpskin, Ploshkin, Pelican jill,
    We think so then, and we thought so still!

Yes, they came; and among the rest,
The King of the Cranes all grandly dressed.
Such a lovely tail! Its feathers float
Between the ends of his blue dress-coat;
With pea-green trowsers all so neat,
And a delicate frill to hide his feet,—
(For though no one speaks of it, every one knows,
He has got no webs between his toes!)
As soon as he saw our Daughter Dell,
In violent love that Crane King fell,—
On seeing her waddling form so fair,
With a wreath of shrimps in her short white hair.
And before the end of the next long day,
Our Dell had given her heart away;
For the King of the Cranes had won that heart,
With a Crocodile's egg and a large fish-tart.
She vowed to marry the King of the Cranes,
Leaving the Nile for stranger plains;
And away they flew in a gathering crowd
Of endless birds in a lengthening cloud.

Ploffskin, Pluffskin, Pelican jee,
We think no Birds so happy as we!
Plumpskin, Ploshkin, Pelican jill,
We think so then, and we thought so still!

And far away in the twilight sky,
We heard them singing a lessening cry,—
Farther and farther till out of sight,
And we stood alone in the silent night!
Often since, in the nights of June,
We sit on the sand and watch the moon;—
She has gone to the great Gromboolian plain,
And we probably never shall meet again!
Oft, in the long still nights of June,
We sit on the rocks and watch the moon;—
—She dwells by the streams of the Chankly Bore,
And we probably never shall see her more.
Ploffskin, Pluffskin, Pelican jee,
We think no Birds so happy as we!
Plumpskin, Ploshkin, Pelican jill,
We think so then, and we thought so still!

6/ *"One of the Dumbs"*

Just as Lear considered himself to be "3 parts crazy," he also found others to be equally odd. "All my friends," he once wrote, "must be fools or mad." In his introduction to *More Nonsense* he explained that he had never "allowed any caricature of private or public persons to appear." Yet, like any writer or artist, he could not help but be influenced by what he saw and experienced.

In his journeys, Lear discovered a host of oddities, from the "cross-leggism" sitting posture of Turks, to a dervish "performing the most wonderful evolutions and gyrations; spinning round and round for his own private diversion, first on his legs and then pivot-wise. . . ." In Albania he commented on a man "who does not indulge in shoes, and I observe that when his hands are occupied, he holds his pipe in his toes, and does any other little office with those, to us, useless members." Women with "their hair tied up in long, caterpillar-like green-silk bags three feet in length" caught his attention, as well as a Lord "who seems to me as if he had dreamed a dream and was continually a-dreaming of having dreamed it." Wearing a single linen garment, "old Sheikh Salah" struck Lear as "a white sack of flour," and he was fascinated by those who walked on stilts, "which mode of progress I mean to learn."

Many of these observations are reflected in the characters who make up "the dumbs."

Manypeeplia Upsidownia

There was an old person of Bar,
Who passed all her life in a jar,
Which she painted pea-green,
To appear more serene,
That placid old person of Bar.

There was an Old Person of Mold,
Who shrank from sensations of cold;
So he purchased some muffs,
Some furs and some fluffs,
And wrapped himself well from the cold.

There was a Young Person of Crete,
Whose toilette was far from complete;
She dressed in a sack,
Spickle-speckled with black,
That ombliferous person of Crete.

There was an Old Man in a tree,
Who was horribly bored by a Bee;
When they said, "Does it buzz?"
He replied, "Yes, it does!
It's a regular brute of a Bee!"

There was an old person of Woking,
Whose mind was perverse and provoking;
He sate on a rail,
With his head in a pail,
That illusive old person of Woking.

There was an Old Person of Spain,
Who hated all trouble and pain;
So he sate on a chair,
With his feet in the air,
That umbrageous Old Person of Spain.

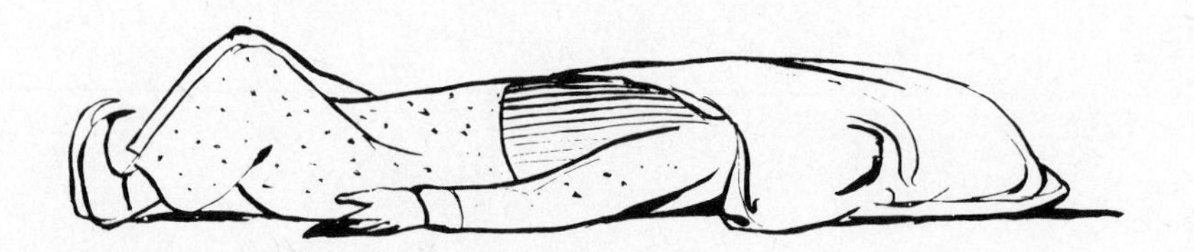

There was an old man of Hong Kong,
Who never did anything wrong;
He lay on his back,
With his head in a sack,
That innocuous old man of Hong Kong.

"One of the Dumbs"

There was an old person of Pinner,
As thin as a lath, if not thinner;
They dressed him in white,
And roll'd him up tight,
That elastic old person of Pinner.

There was an Old Man who said, "Well!
Will *nobody* answer this bell?
I have pulled day and night,
Till my hair has grown white,
But nobody answers this bell!"

There was an old man of Toulouse
Who purchased a new pair of shoes;
When they asked, "Are they pleasant?"—
He said, "Not at present!"
That turbid old man of Toulouse.

There was an old person of Wilts,
Who constantly walked upon stilts;
He wreathed them with lilies,
And daffy-down-dillies,
That elegant person of Wilts.

"One of the Dumbs"

There was an old person of Deal
Who in walking, used only his heel;
    When they said, "Tell us why?"—
    He made no reply;
That mysterious old person of Deal.

There was an Old Man of Melrose,
Who walked on the tips of his toes;
    But they said, "It ain't pleasant,
    To see you at present,
You stupid Old Man of Melrose."

There was an old Man of the Hague,
Whose ideas were excessively vague;
He built a balloon,
To examine the moon,
That deluded Old Man of the Hague.

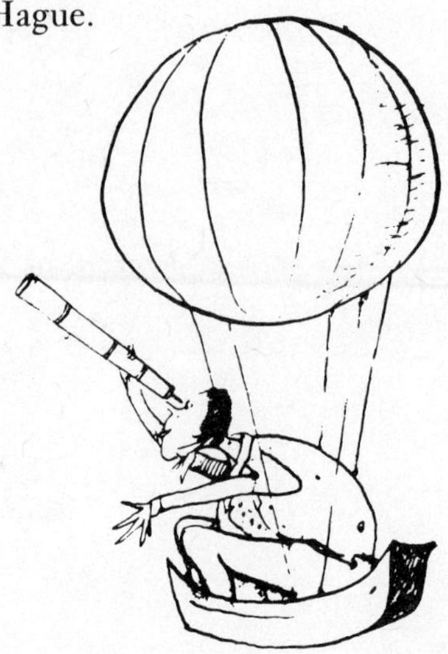

There was an Old Man on a hill,
Who seldom, if ever, stood still;
He ran up and down,
In his Grandmother's gown,
Which adorned that Old Man on a hill.

There was an Old Man of Whitehaven,
Who danced a quadrille with a Raven;
    But they said—"It's absurd,
    To encourage this bird!"
So they smashed that Old Man of Whitehaven.

There was an old lady of France,
Who taught little ducklings to dance;
    When she said, "Tick-a-tack!"—
    They only said, "Quack!"
Which grieved that old lady of France.

There was an old person of Ware,
Who rode on the back of a bear:
When they ask'd,—"Does it trot?"—
He said, "Certainly not!
He's a Moppsikon Floppsikon bear!"

7/ "A Runcible Hat"

Wherever Lear journeyed, he would pay particular attention to the headgear of the people. Traveling in Calabria during a period of political unrest, he noted that "it is only in the provinces of Catanzáro and Cosenza where the real (and awful) pyramidal brigand's hat is adopted," and recorded that his muleteer wore "nothing but a Sicilian long blue cap" which he later referred to as "Sicilian long blue nightcaps."

In Corsica he observed that older women "mostly wear a black handkerchief tied closely over the head; but the younger . . . wear two handkerchiefs, the one tied round the forehead and fastened behind the head (and of this kerchief only a portion of the front is seen), the other over the top of the head, fastened below the chin and falling on the back of the neck in a point like the head-dress represented in old Italian pictures." Here he bemoaned the lack of colorful costumes and recalled the "wood scenes of Eriligove, in Thrace. Would that here there were the village girls of those parts, with their gold and coin chains, their red caps, and their flower festoon'd head-dresses."

In Turkey, the dervishes with "high, white felt, steeple-crowned hats with black shawls around them" and a Turk "with bells on his turban" made a great impression. Certainly "The Quangle Wangle's Hat" with its "ribbons and bibbons on every side/And bells . . ." is a composite of much that he observed.

The Scroobious Snake,
who always wore a Hat on his Head, for
fear he should bite anybody.

The Quangle Wangle's Hat

I

On the top of the Crumpetty Tree
The Quangle Wangle sat,
But his face you could not see,
On account of his Beaver Hat.
For his Hat was a hundred and two feet wide,
With ribbons and bibbons on every side
And bells, and buttons, and loops, and lace,
So that nobody ever could see the face
Of the Quangle Wangle Quee.

II

The Quangle Wangle said
To himself on the Crumpetty Tree,—
"Jam; and jelly; and bread;
Are the best of food for me!
But the longer I live on this Crumpetty Tree
The plainer than ever it seems to me
That very few people come this way
And that life on the whole is far from gay!"
Said the Quangle Wangle Quee.

III

But there came to the Crumpetty Tree,
Mr. and Mrs. Canary;
And they said,—"Did ever you see
Any spot so charmingly airy?
May we build a nest on your lovely Hat?
Mr. Quangle Wangle, grant us that!
O please let us come and build a nest
Of whatever material suits you best,
Mr. Quangle Wangle Quee!"

IV

And besides, to the Crumpetty Tree
Came the Stork, the Duck, and the Owl;
The Snail, and the Bumble-Bee,
The Frog, and the Fimble Fowl;
(The Fimble Fowl, with a Corkscrew leg;)
And all of them said,—"We humbly beg,
We may build our homes on your lovely Hat,—
Mr. Quangle Wangle, grant us that!
Mr. Quangle Wangle Quee!"

V

And the Golden Grouse came there,
 And the Pobble who has no toes,—
And the small Olympian bear,—
 And the Dong with a luminous nose.
And the Blue Baboon, who played the flute,—
And the Orient Calf from the Land of Tute,—
And the Attery Squash, and the Bisky Bat,—
All came and built on the lovely Hat
  Of the Quangle Wangle Quee.

VI

And the Quangle Wangle said
 To himself on the Crumpetty Tree,—
"When all these creatures move
 What a wonderful noise there'll be!"
And at night by the light of the Mulberry moon
They danced to the Flute of the Blue Baboon,
On the broad green leaves of the Crumpetty Tree,
And all were as happy as happy could be,
  With the Quangle Wangle Quee.

"A Runcible Hat"

There was a Young Lady of Dorking,
Who bought a large bonnet for walking;
    But its color and size,
    So bedazzled her eyes,
That she very soon went back to Dorking.

There was an old man of Dee-side
Whose hat was exceedingly wide,
    But he said "Do not fail,
    If it happen to hail
To come under my hat at Dee-side!"

There was a Young Lady whose bonnet,
Came untied when the birds sate upon it;
    But she said, "I don't care!
    All the birds in the air
Are welcome to sit on my bonnet!"

There was a young person in red,
Who carefully covered her head,
    With a bonnet of leather,
    And three lines of feather,
Besides some long ribands of red.

There was an old man on the Border,
Who lived in the utmost disorder;
He danced with the cat,
And made tea in his hat,
Which vexed all the folks on the Border.

There was an old man of Thames Ditton,
Who called out for something to sit on;
But they brought him a hat,
And said—"Sit upon that,
You abruptious old man of Thames Ditton!"

Mr. and Mrs. Spikky Sparrow

I

On a little piece of wood,
Mr. Spikky Sparrow stood;
Mrs. Sparrow sate close by,
A-making of an insect pie,
For her little children five,
In the nest and all alive,
Singing with a cheerful smile
To amuse them all the while,
"Twikky wikky wikky wee,
Wikky bikky twikky tee,
Spikky bikky bee!"

II

Mrs. Spikky Sparrow said,
"Spikky, Darling! in my head
Many thoughts of trouble come,
Like to flies upon a plum!
All last night, among the trees,
I heard you cough, I heard you sneeze;
And thought I, it's come to that
Because he does not wear a hat!
Chippy wippy sikky tee!
Bikky wikky tikky mee!
Spikky chippy wee!

III

Not that you are growing old,
But the nights are growing cold.
No one stays out all night long
Without a hat: I'm sure it's wrong!"
Mr. Spikky said, "How kind,
Dear! you are, to speak your mind!
All your life I wish you luck!
You are, you are, a lovely duck!
Witchy witchy witchy wee!
Twitchy witchy witchy bee!
Tikky tikky tee!

IV

I was also sad, and thinking,
When one day I saw you winking,
And I heard you sniffle-snuffle,
And I saw your feathers ruffle;
To myself I sadly said,
She's neuralgia in her head!
That dear head has nothing on it!
Ought she not to wear a bonnet?
Witchy kitchy kitchy wee?
Spikky wikky mikky bee?
Chippy wippy chee?

V

Let us both fly up to town!
There I'll buy you such a gown!
Which, completely in the fashion,
You shall tie a sky-blue sash on.
And a pair of slippers neat,
To fit your darling little feet,
So that you will look and feel
Quite galloobious and genteel!

Jikky wikky bikky see,
Chicky bikky wikky bee,
Twicky witchy wee!"

VI

So they both to London went,
Alighting on the Monument,
Whence they flew down swiftly—pop!
Into Moses' wholesale shop;
There they bought a hat and bonnet,
And a gown with spots upon it,
A satin sash of Cloxam blue,
And a pair of slippers too.
Zikky wikky mikky bee,
Witchy witchy mitchy kee,
Sikky tikky wee.

VII

Then when so completely drest,
Back they flew, and reached their nest.
Their children cried, "O Ma and Pa!
How truly beautiful you are!"
Said they, "We trust that cold or pain
We shall never feel again!
While, perched on tree, or house, or steeple,
We now shall look like other people.
Witchy witchy witchy wee,
Twikky mikky bikky bee,
Zikky sikky tee."

8/ "He Weeps"

"Perhaps," Lear confided to a friend, "in the next eggzi stens you and I and My Lady may be able to sit for placid hours under a lotus a eating of ice cream and pelican pie, with our feet in a hazure coloured stream and with the birds and beasts of Paradise a sporting around us." Another time he would write, "I wish I was married to a clever good nice fat little Greek girl—and had 25 olive trees, some goats and a house. But the above girl, happily for herself, likes somebody else."

Often these wishes were stripped of their humor. "The only real and proper state of life in this world," he recorded is "if you have a wife, or are in love with a woman." He also would write that "there must be an ideal Mrs. Lear to make up the perfect ideal, & how that is to come about I can't yet tell." But Lear never married, and came to rely upon friendships to stave off his loneliness. "Write upon prawns, rheumatism, Armstrong guns, Birds of Paradise or raspberry jam,—so you write," he told a friend.

"I maintain that those who diminish hope are the worst enemies of humanity—not its friends . . ." he observed. Another time he would explain "that *totally unbroken* application to poetical-topographical painting and drawing is my universal panacea for the ills of life."

And so Lear continued to weave into both his limericks and longer poems both humor and sadness.

Herons and Sweeps,
Turbans and Sheeps,
Set him a weeping
and see how he weeps!

There was an Old Man of Cape Horn,
Who wished he had never been born;
So he sat on a chair,
Till he died of despair,
That dolorous Man of Cape Horn.

There was an old man whose despair
Induced him to purchase a hare:
Whereon one fine day,
He rode wholly away,
Which partly assuaged his despair.

The Courtship of the Yonghy-Bonghy-Bò

I

On the Coast of Coromandel
Where the early pumpkins blow,
In the middle of the woods
  Lived the Yonghy-Bonghy-Bò.
Two old chairs, and half a candle,—
One old jug without a handle,—
    These were all his worldly goods:
    In the middle of the woods,
    These were all the worldly goods,
  Of the Yonghy-Bonghy-Bò,
  Of the Yonghy-Bonghy-Bò.

II

Once, among the Bong-trees walking
  Where the early pumpkins blow,
    To a little heap of stones
  Came the Yonghy-Bonghy-Bò.
There he heard a Lady talking,
To some milk-white Hens of Dorking,—
    "Tis the Lady Jingly Jones!
    On that little heap of stones
    Sits the Lady Jingly Jones!"
  Said the Yonghy-Bonghy-Bò,
  Said the Yonghy-Bonghy-Bò.

III

"Lady Jingly! Lady Jingly!
  Sitting where the pumpkins blow,
    Will you come and be my wife?"
  Said the Yonghy-Bonghy-Bò.
"I am tired of living singly,—
On this coast so wild and shingly,—
    I'm a-weary of my life:
    If you'll come and be my wife,
    Quite serene would be my life!"—
  Said the Yonghy-Bonghy-Bò,
  Said the Yonghy-Bonghy-Bò.

IV

"On this Coast of Coromandel,
  Shrimps and watercresses grow,
    Prawns are plentiful and cheap,"
  Said the Yonghy-Bonghy-Bò.
"You shall have my Chairs and candle,
And my jug without a handle!—
    Gaze upon the rolling deep
    (Fish is plentiful and cheap)
    As the sea, my love is deep!"
  Said the Yonghy-Bonghy-Bò,
  Said the Yonghy-Bonghy-Bò.

V

Lady Jingly answered sadly,
  And her tears began to flow,—
    "Your proposal comes too late,
  Mr. Yonghy-Bonghy-Bò!
I would be your wife most gladly!"
(Here she twirled her fingers madly,)
    "But in England I've a mate!
    Yes! you've asked me far too late,
    For in England I've a mate,
  Mr. Yonghy-Bonghy-Bò!
  Mr. Yonghy-Bonghy-Bò!"

VI

"Mr. Jones—(his name is Handel,—
Handel Jones, Esquire, & Co.)
Dorking fowls delights to send,
Mr. Yonghy-Bonghy-Bò!
Keep, oh! keep your chairs and candle,
And your jug without a handle,—
I can merely be your friend!
—Should my Jones more Dorkings send,
I will give you three, my friend!
Mr. Yonghy-Bonghy-Bò!
Mr. Yonghy-Bonghy-Bò!"

VII

"Though you've such a tiny body,
And your head so large doth grow,—
Though your hat may blow away,
Mr. Yonghy-Bonghy-Bò!
Though you're such a Hoddy-Doddy,
Yet I wish that I could modi-
fy the words I needs must say!
Will you please to go away
That is all I have to say,
Mr. Yonghy-Bonghy-Bò!
Mr. Yonghy-Bonghy-Bò!"

VIII

Down the slippery slopes of Myrtle,
Where the early pumpkins blow,
To the calm and silent sea
Fled the Yonghy-Bonghy-Bò.
There, beyond the Bay of Gurtle,
Lay a large and lively Turtle.
"You're the Cove," he said, "for me;
On your back beyond the sea,
Turtle, you shall carry me!"
Said the Yonghy-Bonghy-Bò,
Said the Yonghy-Bonghy-Bò.

IX

Through the silent-roaring ocean
  Did the Turtle swiftly go;
    Holding fast upon his shell
  Rode the Yonghy-Bonghy-Bò.
With a sad primæval motion
Towards the sunset isles of Boshen
    Still the Turtle bore him well.
    Holding fast upon his shell,
    "Lady Jingly Jones, farewell!"
  Sang the Yonghy-Bonghy-Bò,
  Sang the Yonghy-Bonghy-Bò.

X

From the Coast of Coromandel,
  Did that Lady never go;
    On that heap of stones she mourns
  For the Yonghy-Bonghy-Bò.
On that Coast of Coromandel,
In his jug without a handle
    Still she weeps, and daily moans;
    On that little heap of stones
    To her Dorking Hens she moans,
  For the Yonghy-Bonghy-Bò,
  For the Yonghy-Bonghy-Bò.

The Yonghy-Bonghy-Bò,
whose Head was ever so much bigger than his
Body, and whose Hat was rather small.

Calico Pie

I

Calico Pie,
The little Birds fly
Down to the calico tree,
Their wings were blue,
And they sang "Tilly-loo!"
Till away they flew,—
And they never came back to me!
They never came back!
They never came back!
They never came back to me!

II

Calico Jam,
The little Fish swam,
Over the syllabub sea,
He took off his hat,

To the Sole and the Sprat,
And the Willeby-wat,—
But he never came back to me!

He never came back!
He never came back!
He never came back to me!

III

Calico Ban,
The little Mice ran,
To be ready in time for tea,
Flippity flup,
They drank it all up,
And danced in the cup,—

But they never came back to me!
They never came back!
They never came back!
They never came back to me!

IV

Calico Drum,
The Grasshoppers come,
The Butterfly, Beetle, and Bee,

Over the ground,
Around and round,
With a hop and a bound,—

But they never came back!
They never came back!
They never came back!
They never came back to me!

There was a Young Lady of Turkey,
Who wept when the weather was murky;
When the day turned out fine,
She ceased to repine,
That capricious Young Lady of Turkey.

There was an Old Man of Bohemia,
Whose daughter was christened Euphemia;
    But one day, to his grief,
    She married a thief,
Which grieved that Old Man of Bohemia.

There was an old person of Pett,
Who was partly consumed by regret;
    He sate in a cart,
    And ate cold apple tart,
Which relieved that old person of Pett.

Incidents in the Life of My Uncle Arly

I

O My agèd Uncle Arly!
Sitting on a heap of Barley
Thro' the silent hours of night,—
Close beside a leafy thicket:—
On his nose there was a Cricket,—
In his hat a Railway-Ticket;—
(But his shoes were far too tight.)

II

Long ago, in youth, he squander'd
All his goods away, and wander'd
To the Tiniskoop-hills afar.
There on golden sunsets blazing,
Every evening found him gazing,—
Singing,—"Orb! you're quite amazing!
How I wonder what you are!"

III

Like the ancient Medes and Persians,
Always by his own exertions
He subsisted on those hills;—
Whiles,—by teaching children spelling,—
Or at times by merely yelling,—
Or at intervals by selling
"Propter's Nicodemus Pills."

IV

Later, in his morning rambles
He perceived the moving brambles—
Something square and white disclose;—
'Twas a First-class Railway-Ticket;
But, on stooping down to pick it
Off the ground,—a pea-green Cricket
Settled on my uncle's Nose.

V

Never—never more,—oh! never,
Did that Cricket leave him ever,—
Dawn or evening, day or night;—
Clinging as a constant treasure,—
Chirping with a cheerious measure,—
Wholly to my uncle's pleasure,—
(Though his shoes were far too tight.)

VI

So for three-and-forty winters,
Till his shoes were worn to splinters,
All those hills he wander'd o'er,—
Sometimes silent;—sometimes yelling;—
Till he came to Borley-Melling,
Near his old ancestral dwelling;—
(But his shoes were far too tight.)

VII

On a little heap of Barley
Died my agèd uncle Arly,
And they buried him one night;—
Close beside the leafy thicket;—
There,—his hat and Railway-Ticket;—
There,—his ever-faithful Cricket;—
(But his shoes were far too tight.)

9/ *"By the Side of the Ocean"*

Lear liked to "puddle along the shingly beach" in Rome, observe the "pomskizillious and gromphibberous" coastal scenery on the island of Gozo, view from a room at his home, Villa Emily, "the syllabub sea and the obvious octagonal ocean."

Sea, ocean and river captivated his imagination, yet often he likened their desolation to his own state of mind. "Most lonely, lonely river!," he wrote of the Nile, "the intense loneliness of the river." The Owl and the Pussy-Cat could dance "hand in hand, on the edge of the sand," yet Lear often saw himself "on the bleak shore, alone."

A number of limerick characters delight in sailing off to sea in strange craft. The Pobble happily swims the Bristol Channel. Travel by water, with its attendant hopes of change and delight were as much a part of Lear's life as those of the characters he created.

"By the Side of the Ocean"

There was an old person of Bree,
Who frequented the depths of the sea;
She nurs'd the small fishes,
And washed all the dishes,
And swam back again into Bree.

There was an Old Person of Ems,
Who casually fell in the Thames;
And when he was found,
They said he was drowned,
That unlucky Old Person of Ems.

There was an old person of Grange,
Whose manners were scroobious and strange;
He sailed to St. Blubb,
In a waterproof tub,
That aquatic old person of Grange.

There was an old man of Dunluce,
Who went out to sea on a goose:
When he'd gone out a mile,
He observ'd with a smile,
"It is time to return to Dunluce."

There was a Young Lady of Portugal,
Whose ideas were excessively nautical:
She climbed up a tree,
To examine the sea,
But declared she would never leave Portugal.

There was an old person of Hyde,
Who walked by the shore with his bride,
Till a Crab who came near,
Fill'd their bosoms with fear,
And they said, "Would we'd never left Hyde!"

There was a Young Lady of Wales,
Who caught a large Fish without scales;
When she lifted her hook,
She exclaimed, "Only look!"
That ecstatic Young Lady of Wales.

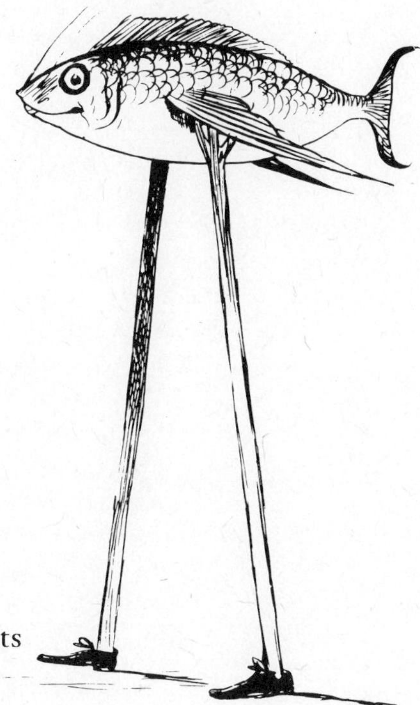

The Fizzgiggious Fish,
who always walked about upon Stilts
because he had no legs.

The Owl and the Pussy-Cat

I

The Owl and the Pussy-cat went to sea
In a beautiful pea-green boat,
They took some honey, and plenty of money,
Wrapped up in a five-pound note.
The Owl looked up to the stars above,
And sang to a small guitar,
"O lovely Pussy! O Pussy, my love,
What a beautiful Pussy you are,
You are,
You are!
What a beautiful Pussy you are!"

II

Pussy said to the Owl, "You elegant fowl!
How charmingly sweet you sing!
O let us be married! too long we have tarried:
But what shall we do for a ring?"
They sailed away, for a year and a day,
To the land where the Bong-tree grows
And there in a wood a Piggy-wig stood
With a ring at the end of his nose,
His nose,
His nose,
With a ring at the end of his nose.

III

"Dear Pig, are you willing to sell for one shilling
Your ring?" Said the Piggy, "I will."
So they took it away, and were married next day
By the Turkey who lives on the hill.
They dined on mince, and slices of quince,
Which they ate with a runcible spoon;
And hand in hand, on the edge of the sand,
They danced by the light of the moon,
The moon,
The moon,
They danced by the light of the moon.

10/ "*Pancakes and . . . Chocolate Shrimps*"

Lear's love of food is recorded in letters, diaries and journals. He might describe a dinner of soup, fish, a beefsteak pudding, woodcock and apple pie to his sister Ann, but pelican pies, Parrot pudding, Lizard Lozenges and Ambeleboff pies were served in his imaginary world. "I have ordered," he wrote to a friend when he was ill, "a baked Barometer for dinner, and 2 Thermometers stewed in treacle for supper." Traveling in Greece with his servant Giorgio and running short of food, he speculated "how Giorgio should cook the large blue jelly fish that the sea threw up. We found 2 small crabs also—& I proposed—as there were blackberries all about, to boil the jelly fish with blackberry sauce and to roast the crabs with rhum & bread crumbs—a triumph of cookery. . . ."

The odd foods consumed by his limerick characters might be explained, in part, by a journal entry of 1851. "We halted," Lear wrote, "close to a little stream full of capital water cresses which I began to gather and eat with some bread and cheese, an act which provoked the Epirote bystanders of the village to extatic laughter and curiosity. Every portion I put into my mouth, delighted them as a most charming exhibition of foreign whim; and the more juvenile spectators instantly commenced bringing me all sorts of funny objects, with an earnest request that [I] would amuse them by feeding thereupon forthwith. One brought a thistle, a second a collection of sticks and wood, a third some grass; a fourth presented me with a fat grasshopper—the whole scene was acted amid shouts of laughter, in which I joined as loudly as any."

It is little wonder that Lear would use this idea as a basis for nonsense ever afterwards!

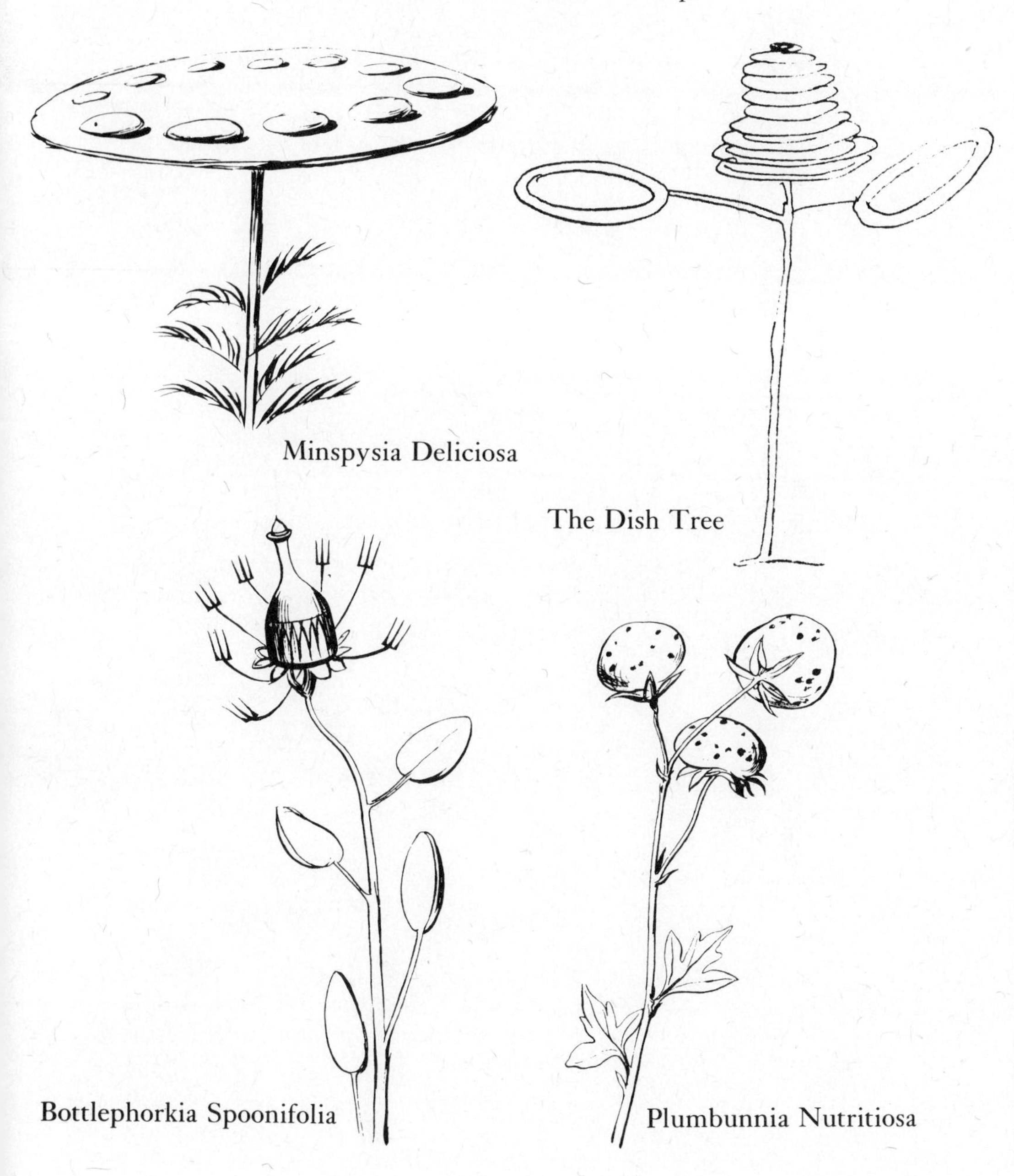
Minspysia Deliciosa
The Dish Tree
Bottlephorkia Spoonifolia
Plumbunnia Nutritiosa

There was an old Person whose habits,
Induced him to feed upon Rabbits;
When he'd eaten eighteen,
He turned perfectly green,
Upon which he relinquished those habits.

There was an Old Man of Calcutta,
Who perpetually ate bread and butter;
Till a great bit of muffin,
On which he was stuffing,
Choked that horrid old man of Calcutta.

There was an old person of Fife,
Who was greatly disgusted with life;
They sang him a ballad,
And fed him on salad,
Which cured that old person of Fife.

There was an old person of Dean
Who dined on one pea, and one bean;
For he said, "More than that,
Would make me too fat,"
That cautious old person of Dean.

There was an old man of El Hums,
Who lived upon nothing but crumbs,
    Which he picked off the ground,
    With the other birds round,
In the roads and the lanes of El Hums.

There was an Old Man of Apulia,
Whose conduct was very peculiar
    He fed twenty sons,
    Upon nothing but buns,
That whimsical Man of Apulia.

Nonsense Cookery

Extract from the *Nonsense Gazette*, for August 1870.

Our readers will be interested in the following communications from our valued and learned contributor, Professor Bosh, whose labours in the fields of Culinary and Botanical science, are so well known to all the world. The first three Articles richly merit to be added to the Domestic cookery of every family; those which follow, claim the attention of all Botanists, and we are happy to be able through Dr. Bosh's kindness to present our readers with illustrations of his discoveries. All the new flowers are found in the valley of Verrikwier, near the lake of Oddgrow, and on the summit of the hill Orfeltugg.

Three Receipts for Domestic Cookery

TO MAKE AN AMBLONGUS PIE

Take 4 pounds (say 4½ pounds) of fresh Amblongusses, and put them in a small pipkin.

Cover them with water and boil them for 8 hours incessantly, after which add 2 pints of new milk, and proceed to boil for 4 hours more.

When you have ascertained that the Amblongusses are quite soft, take them out and place them in a wide pan, taking care to shake them well previously.

Grate some nutmeg over the surface, and cover them carefully with powdered gingerbread, curry-powder, and a sufficient quantity of Cayenne pepper.

Remove the pan into the next room, and place it on the floor. Bring it back again, and let it simmer for three-quarters of an hour. Shake the pan violently till all the Amblongusses have become of a pale purple color.

Then, having prepared the paste, insert the whole carefully, adding at the same time a small pigeon, 2 slices of beef, 4 cauliflowers, and any number of oysters.

Watch patiently till the crust begins to rise, and add a pinch of salt from time to time.

Serve up in a clean dish, and throw the whole out of window as fast as possible.

TO MAKE CRUMBOBBLIOUS CUTLETS

Procure some strips of beef, and having cut them into the smallest possible slices, proceed to cut them still smaller, eight or perhaps nine times.

When the whole is thus minced, brush it up hastily with a new clothes-brush, and stir round rapidly and capriciously with a salt-spoon or a soup-ladle.

Place the whole in a saucepan, and remove it to a sunny place,—say the roof of the house if free from sparrows or other birds,—and leave it there for about a week.

At the end of that time add a little lavender, some oil of almonds, and a few herring-bones; and then cover the whole with 4 gallons of clarified crumbobblious sauce, when it will be ready for use.

Cut it into the shape of ordinary cutlets, and serve up in a clean tablecloth or dinner-napkin.

TO MAKE GOSKY PATTIES

Take a Pig, three or four years of age, and tie him by the off-hind leg to a post. Place 5 pounds of currants, 3 of sugar, 2 pecks of peas, 18 roast chestnuts, a candle, and six bushels of turnips, within his reach; if he eats these, constantly provide him with more.

Then procure some cream, some slices of Cheshire cheese, four quires of foolscap paper, and a packet of black pins. Work the whole into a paste, and spread it out to dry on a sheet of clean brown water-proof linen.

When the paste is perfectly dry, but not before, proceed to beat the Pig violently, with the handle of a large broom. If he squeals, beat him again.

Visit the paste and beat the Pig alternately for some days, and ascertain if at the end of that period the whole is about to turn into Gosky Patties.

If it does not then, it never will; and in that case the Pig may be let loose, and the whole process may be considered as finished.

Tureenia Ladlecum

There was an Old Person of Chili,
Whose conduct was painful and silly;
He sate on the stairs,
Eating apples and pears,
That imprudent Old Person of Chili.

There was a young lady of Greenwich,
Whose garments were border'd with Spinach;
But a large spotty Calf
Bit her shawl quite in half,
Which alarmed that young lady of Greenwich.

There was an Old Person of Hurst,
Who drank when he was not athirst;
When they said, "You'll grow fatter,"
He answered, "What matter?"
That globular Person of Hurst.

There was a Young Lady of Poole,
Whose soup was excessively cool;
So she put it to boil
By the aid of some oil,
That ingenious Young Lady of Poole.

There was an old man of Dumbree,
Who taught little owls to drink tea;
For he said, "To eat mice,
Is not proper or nice,"
That amiable man of Dumbree.

There was an Old Person of Ewell,
Who chiefly subsisted on gruel;
But to make it more nice,
He inserted some Mice,
Which refreshed that Old Person of Ewell.

There was an Old Man of Kilkenny,
Who never had more than a penny;
He spent all the money
In onions and honey,
That wayward Old Man of Kilkenny.

There was an Old Person of Rheims,
Who was troubled with horrible dreams;
So to keep him awake
They fed him with cake,
Which amused that Old Person of Rheims.

11/ *"The Days of His Pilgrimage"*

"If you are absolutely alone in the world, & likely to be so," Lear wrote, "then move about continually & never stand still." Always in search of "constantly new and burningly bright scenes" and "grisogorious places" he journeyed in Italy, Greece, Turkey, Albania, Lebanon, Egypt, Palestine, Switzerland, France, India and Ceylon. He traveled by foot, by mule, horse and camel, by "fuliginious flea-full steamer" and by "long continuance of railway travel" which "plays the deuce with my irritable body & mind."

Yet he kept on moving, enduring the "terror and disgust" of a sea passage, or the "brutal railway." He described the "long and hardish work" of packing and unpacking, of setting up "eggzibissions" in order to sell his paintings and to earn enough money to live and travel further. "What to do? *What* I say to do," he wrote in his diary, "To stay here? to go *where?*" In a humorous mood he would contemplate a trip "either to Sardinia, or India, or Jumsibojiggle quack" or to a "piggywiggy island."

Many of the nonsense characters he created, the Duck and the Kangaroo, the Table and the Chair, the Jumblies and others also traveled. Some ventured only a few miles from home but others found the Torrible Zone, the Hills of the Chankly Bore and "hopped the world three times round."

In the end, however, they returned home, as did Edward Lear whose last days were spent at Villa Emily in San Remo. He died on January 29, 1888, "the days of his pilgrimage" ended.

The Table and the Chair

I

Said the Table to the Chair,
"You can hardly be aware,
How I suffer from the heat,
And from chilblains on my feet!
If we took a little walk,
We might have a little talk!
Pray let us take the air!"
Said the Table to the Chair.

II

Said the Chair unto the Table,
"Now you *know* we are not able!
How foolishly you talk,
When you know we *cannot* walk!"
Said the Table, with a sigh,
"It can do no harm to try,
I've as many legs as you,
Why can't we walk on two?"

III

So they both went slowly down,
And walked about the town
With a cheerful bumpy sound,
As they toddled round and round.

And everybody cried,
As they hastened to their side
"See! the Table and the Chair
Have come out to take the air!"

IV

But in going down an alley,
To a castle in a valley,
They completely lost their way,
And wandered all the day,

Till, to see them safely back,
They paid a Ducky-quack,
And a Beetle, and a Mouse,
Who took them to their house.

V

Then they whispered to each other,
"O delightful little brother!
What a lovely walk we've taken!
Let us dine on Beans and Bacon!"
So the Ducky, and the leetle
Browny-Mousy and the Beetle
Dined, and danced upon their heads
Till they toddled to their beds.

The Duck and the Kangaroo

I

Said the Duck to the Kangaroo,
"Good gracious! how you hop!
Over the fields and the water too,
As if you never would stop!
My life is a bore in this nasty pond,
And I long to go out in the world beyond!
I wish I could hop like you!"
Said the Duck to the Kangaroo.

II

"Please give me a ride on your back!"
Said the Duck to the Kangaroo.
"I would sit quite still, and say nothing but 'Quack,'
The whole of the long day through!
And we'd go to the Dee, and the Jelly Bo Lee,
Over the land, and over the sea;—
Please take me a ride! O do!"
Said the Duck to the Kangaroo.

III

Said the Kangaroo to the Duck,
  "This requires some little reflection;
Perhaps on the whole it might bring me luck,
  And there seems but one objection,
Which is, if you'll let me speak so bold,
Your feet are unpleasantly wet and cold,
And would probably give me the roo-
  Matiz!" said the Kangaroo.

IV

Said the Duck, "As I sate on the rocks,
  I have thought over that completely,
And I bought four pairs of worsted socks
  Which fit my web-feet neatly.
And to keep out the cold I've bought a cloak,
And every day a cigar I'll smoke,
  All to follow my own dear true
  Love of a Kangaroo!"

V

Said the Kangaroo, "I'm ready!
  All in the moonlight pale;
But to balance me well, dear Duck, sit steady!
  And quite at the end of my tail!"
So away they went with a hop and a bound,
And they hopped the whole world three times round;
  And who so happy,—O who,
  As the Duck and the Kangaroo?.

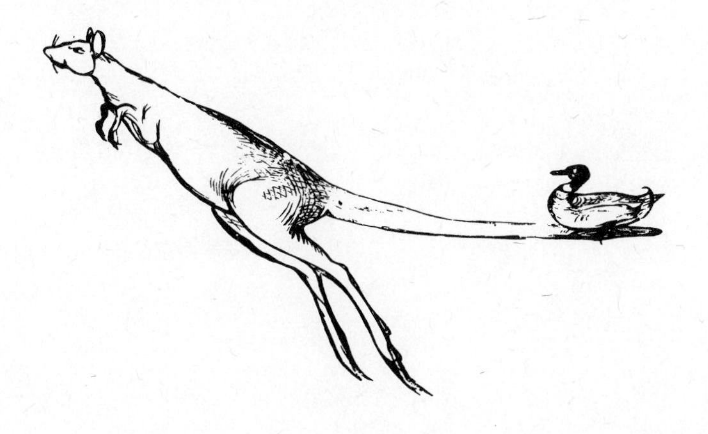

The Zigzag Zealous Zebra,
who carried five Monkeys on his back all
the way to Jellibolee.

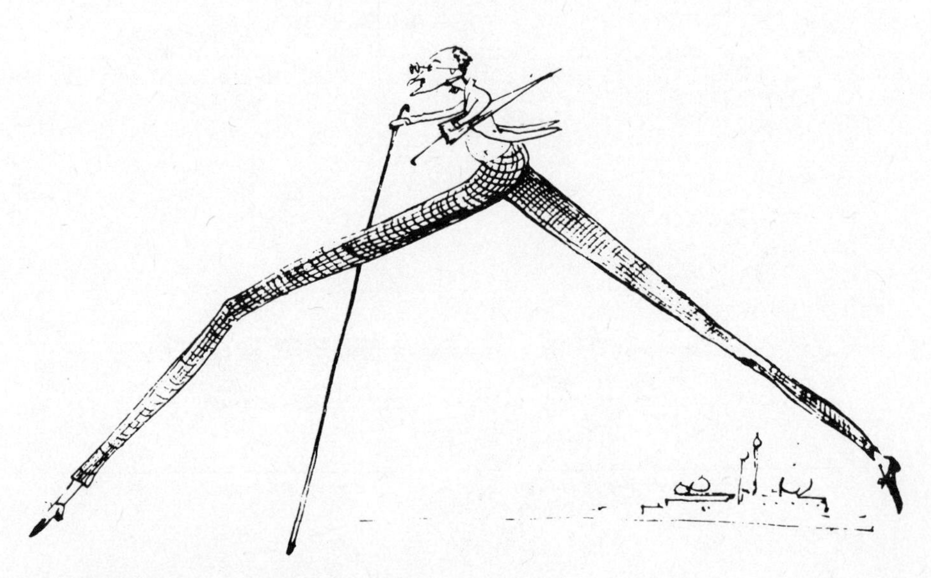

There was an Old Man of Coblenz,
The length of whose legs was immense;
He went with one prance,
From Turkey to France,
That surprising Old Man of Coblenz.

There was an Old Person of Gretna,
Who rushed down the crater of Etna;
When they said, "Is it hot?"
He replied, "No, it's not!"
That mendacious Old Person of Gretna.

There was an Old Man at a Junction,
Whose feelings were wrung with compunction,
When they said "The Train's gone!"
He exclaimed "How forlorn!"
But remained on the rails of the Junction.

There was an Old Person of Philœ,
Whose conduct was scroobious and wily;
He rushed up a Palm,
When the weather was calm,
And observed all the ruins of Philœ.

The Jumblies

I

They went to sea in a Sieve, they did,
  In a Sieve they went to sea:
In spite of all their friends could say,
On a winter's morn, on a stormy day,
  In a Sieve they went to sea!
And when the Sieve turned round and round,
And every one cried, "You'll all be drowned!"
They called aloud, "Our Sieve ain't big,
But we don't care a button! we don't care a fig!
  In a Sieve we'll go to sea!"
    Far and few, far and few,
      Are the lands where the Jumblies live;
    Their heads are green, and their hands are blue,
      And they went to sea in a Sieve.

II

They sailed away in a Sieve, they did,
  In a Sieve they sailed so fast,
With only a beautiful pea-green veil
Tied with a riband by way of a sail,
  To a small tobacco-pipe mast;
And every one said, who saw them go,
"O won't they be soon upset, you know!

For the sky is dark, and the voyage is long,
And happen what may, it's extremely wrong
In a Sieve to sail so fast!"
Far and few, far and few,
Are the lands where the Jumblies live;
Their heads are green, and their hands are blue,
And they went to sea in a Sieve.

III

The water it soon came in, it did,
The water it soon came in;
So to keep them dry, they wrapped their feet
In a pinky paper all folded neat,
And they fastened it down with a pin.
And they passed the night in a crockery-jar,
And each of them said, "How wise we are!
Though the sky be dark, and the voyage be long,
Yet we never can think we were rash or wrong,
While round in our Sieve we spin!"
Far and few, far and few,
Are the lands where the Jumblies live;
Their heads are green, and their hands are blue,
And they went to sea in a Sieve.

IV

And all night long they sailed away;
And when the sun went down,
They whistled and warbled a moony song
To the echoing sound of a coppery gong,
In the shade of the mountains brown.
"O Timballo! How happy we are,
When we live in a sieve and a crockery-jar,
And all night long in the moonlight pale,
We sail away with a pea-green sail,
In the shade of the mountains brown!"

Far and few, far and few,
Are the lands where the Jumblies live;
Their heads are green, and their hands are blue,
And they went to sea in a Sieve.

V

They sailed to the Western Sea, they did,
To a land all covered with trees,
And they bought an Owl, and a useful Cart,
And a pound of Rice, and a Cranberry Tart,
And a hive of silvery Bees.
And they bought a Pig, and some green Jack-daws,
And a lovely Monkey with lollipop paws,
And forty bottles of Ring-Bo-Ree,
And no end of Stilton Cheese.
Far and few, far and few,
Are the lands where the Jumblies live;
Their heads are green, and their hands are blue,
And they went to sea in a Sieve.

VI

And in twenty years they all came back,
In twenty years or more,
And every one said, "How tall they've grown!
For they've been to the Lakes, and the Torrible Zone,
And the hills of the Chankly Bore;"
And they drank their health, and gave them a feast
Of dumplings made of beautiful yeast;
And every one said, "If we only live,
We too will go to sea in a Sieve,—
To the hills of the Chankly Bore!"
Far and few, far and few,
Are the lands where the Jumblies live;
Their heads are green, and their hands are blue,
And they went to sea in a Sieve.

Notes on the Sources of the Poems, Further Fax & Speculations About Old Derry down Derry

A Book of Nonsense

Published in 1846, *A Book of Nonsense* by Derry down Derry contained seventy limericks in two volumes, with a limerick on the title page:

> There was an Old Derry down Derry,
> Who loved to see little folks merry;
> So he made them a book
> And with laughter they shook
> At the fun of that Derry down Derry.

Lear used the pseudonym of Derry down Derry in 1846, but when the new and enlarged edition was published in 1861 it bore his own name. For this new edition Lear added forty-two limericks. The book was dedicated "To the great-grandchildren, grand-nephews, and grand-nieces of Edward, 13th Earl of Derby" with the added notation that the "greater part" of the drawings and verses were "originally made and composed for their parents."

Writing to his friend Chichester Fortescue in October 1861, Lear explained that "*All* the nonsense book, with 42 additional illustrations are completed as woodcuts, & negrotiations commence with a Buplisher next week." Ten years later, in a letter to Lady Waldgrave he expressed delight in discovering that in reading letters he had sent to his sister while at Knowsley, he was reminded of those earlier days: "My descriptions at Knowsley choke me with laughter."

Included in this book are fifty limericks from both the 1846 and 1861 editions. These are the persons of Anerley, Apulia, Bangor, Bohemia, Bute, Calcutta, Cape Horn, Chili, Coblenz, Crete, Dorking, Dutton, Ems, Ewell, Gretna, the Hague, Hurst, the Isles, Kilkenny, Melrose, Mold, Peru, Philœ, Poole, Portugal, Rheims, South, Spain, Tring, Turkey, Tyre, Wales, Welling, West and Whitehaven. Others include beard, beard, bonnet, chin, eyes, flute, gong, habits, hill, "Hush!," nose, nose, nose, tree and "Well!."

NONSENSE SONGS, STORIES, BOTANY, AND ALPHABETS

"Now I finish 3 Alphabets for children—and so get pretty wearied at end of the week," Lear wrote to Fortescue in February 1858. The next year, imitating the style of Arthur Clough, a popular poet of the day, he wrote:

> A week or month hence, I will find time to make a
> queer Alphabet,
> All with the letters beversed, and be-aided with pictures,
> Which I shall give—(but don't tell him just yet) to
> Charles Braham's little one.

From Corfu, in 1863, Lear again told Fortescue that "Nonsense issues from me at times—to make a new book next year"; and in 1867 he wrote from London that "Sometimes I make considerable progress in my new Book of Nonsense."

The book, containing nine Nonsense Songs, two Nonsense Stories, Nonsense Cookery, Nonsense Botany and three Nonsense Alphabets was published in 1871. Of the songs, six are included in this selection: "The Owl and the Pussy-Cat," "The Duck and the Kangaroo," "The Jumblies," "Calico Pie," "Mr. and Mrs. Spikky Sparrow" and "The Table and the Chair."

"BOTTLEPHORKIA SPOONIFOLIA"

This drawing from "Nonsense Botany" is one of the drawings Lear did for Daisy Crawford during the summer of 1870 when he was staying at La Certosa del Pesio, a hotel near Turin. Inspired by the strange dishes and unusual cutlery of the *table d'hote,* Lear amused Daisy, her sister Mary and the Terry children with alphabets, poems and drawings.

Neither Lear nor the children liked the convention of the *table d'hote,* an arrangement whereby a prearranged menu is served at a specific hour at a fixed price. Lear's "Nonsense Cookery," also written for Daisy, was certainly a result of their mutual rebellion against the eating provisions.

Other selections from "Nonsense Botany" which appear in this book are "Fishia Marina," "Guittara Pensilis," "Manypeeplia Upsidownia," "Phattfacia Stupenda" and "Plumbunnia Nutritiosa." These drawings and "Nonsense Cookery" appeared in *Nonsense Songs, Stories, Botany, and Alphabets,* published in 1871.

"THE DUCK AND THE KANGAROO"

This was first published in an American magazine, *Young Folks,* in 1870 and appeared a year later in *Nonsense Songs, Stories, Botany, and Alphabets.*

"THE OWL AND THE PUSSY-CAT"

Written for Janet Symonds, daughter of his friend John Addington Symonds, this is one of the poems set to music by Lear. Margaret Terry (later Mrs. Winthrop Chanler) recalled how he sang it to her "to a funny little crooning tune of his own composition" in the summer of 1870. It was one of the songs he played and sang for the Bevan family in 1879.

First published in *Young Folks*, an American magazine, in 1870, it was included in *Nonsense Songs, Stories, Botany, and Alphabets* in 1871.

MORE NONSENSE, PICTURES, RHYMES, BOTANY, ETC.

"Speaking of bosh," Lear wrote to Fortescue on September 13, 1871, "I have done another whole book of it; it is to be called 'MORE NONSENSE' and Bush brings it out at Xmas: *it will have a portrait of me outside.* I should have liked to dedicate it to you, but I thought it was not dignified enough for a Cabinet M.[inister]."

Lear wrote an introduction for this book, explaining how he had claimed authorship of the book as he overheard an "old gentleman" in a railway carriage exclaim that "no such person as 'Edward Lear' exists!" The contents of the book, he wrote, were "made at different intervals in the last two years." He further wished to assure his readers that he was the author of *A Book of Nonsense;* that "every one of the Rhymes was composed by myself, and every one of the Illustrations drawn by my own hand at the time the verses were made." Old Derry down Derry was not, as some thought, the Earl of Derby, but Lear, and he wished to lay this "absurd report" to rest.

The book contained one set of "Nonsense Botany" drawings, of which "Minspysia Deliciosa" is included in the present selection. "26 Nonsense Pictures and Rhymes," often called "The Absolutely Abstemious Ass" alphabet, and one hundred limericks of which fifty are reprinted here. These are the persons of Ayr, Bar, Blackheath, the Border, Bree, Brigg, Bromley, Bude, Cassel, Crowle, Deal, Dean, Dee-side, Down, Dumblane, Dumbree, Dunluce, Dunrose, El Hums, Fife, Filey, Firle, France, Grange, Greenwich, Hong Kong, Hyde, Ibreem, Jodd, a Marsh, Messina, Newry, Nice, Pett, Pinner, Sestri, Skye, Thames Ditton, Toulouse, Ware, West Dumpet, Wilts and Woking. Others include a barge, despair, green, a Junction, nose, red and tree.

"26 Nonsense Pictures and Rhymes"

Written during the summer of 1870 at the hotel, La Certosa del Pesio, near Turin, Lear created this alphabet for a little American girl, Margaret Terry, and her brother Arthur. Each day they would find a letter of the alphabet on their luncheon plate. It was "beautifully drawn in pen and ink and delicately tinted in water-colours," she recalled in her book *Roman Spring*, "done on odd scraps of paper, backs of letters and discarded manuscript." The last part of the work to be presented was the title page with a portrait of a smiling, spectacled Lear portrayed as the "Adopty Duncle."

Published in *More Nonsense* (1872), and known now as "The Absolutely Abstemious Ass" alphabet, ten selections appear in this book including "The Fizzgiggious Fish," "The Judicious Jubilant Jay," "The Melodious Meritorious Mouse," "The Rural Runcible Raven," "The Scroobious Snake," "The Tumultuous Tom-tommy Tortoise," "The Umbrageous Umbrella-maker," "The Worrying Whizzing Wasp," "The Yonghy-Bonghy-Bò" and "The Zigzag Zealous Zebra."

Laughable Lyrics: A Fourth Book of Nonsense Poems, Songs, Botany, Music &c.

This was the last of the nonsense books published by Lear during his lifetime and appeared in 1877. It contained ten poems of which five appear in this selection. These are "The Dong with the Luminous Nose," "The Pelican Chorus," "The Courtship of the Yonghy-Bonghy-Bò," "The Pobble Who Has No Toes," and "The Quangle Wangle's Hat."

Of the ten "New Nonsense Botany" drawings, two are included in this book, "Crabbia Horrida" and "Tureenia Ladlecum."

"The Courtship of the Yonghy-Bonghy-Bò"

In July of 1847 Lear journeyed through southern Calabria. The guide who served him "answered only in sentences ending with—'Dogo, dighi, doghi, daghi, da' in Calabrese lingo. "What the 'Dogo' was we never knew," Lear wrote in his journal, "though it was the object of our keenest search throughout the tour to ascertain if it were animal, mineral or vegetable." Each "unintelligible" sentence ended in "Dighi doghi Da," a phrase Lear's biographers feel formed the metrical basis for his Yonghy-Bonghy-Bò.

Lear's journals contain another entry just as germane to the origin of the name. On October 22, 1848, traveling in Greece, Lear wrote about a performing gypsy who sang to a "frantic harmony—'Bo, bo-bo-bo, bo-bo-bo, bo-bo-bo, bo-bo-bo, bobobo BO!'—the last 'BO' uttered like a pistol-shot, and followed by an unanimous yell."

Certainly both of these experiences might have stayed in Lear's mind; during the summer of 1870 the American girl, Margaret Terry, remembered how she and Lear kicked chestnut balls, calling them "yonghy bonghy bos." Lear finished the poem in 1871 and wrote to a friend "how nicely" Henry Strachey "would repeat a poem I have lately made on the Yonghy Bonghy Bò." Earlier that year he had written to his friend Fortescue about a ballad he had done "on the 'Yonghy Bonghy Bò' which (and its music) makes a furore here. I shall ask Bush if single ballads can be brought out, or two or three at a time. . . ." In 1876 he wrote to Fortescue, now Lord Carlingford: "If you are in Bush's shop, ask him to show you a poem about 'Lady Jingly Jones,' it comes out in a new edition of 'Nonsense Songs and Stories' later. . . ."

"The Courtship of the Yonghy-Bonghy-Bò" appeared in *Laughable Lyrics* in 1877, and was thought by many to be anything but "laughable." It is one of those poems Lear set to music and played for the Bevan family in 1879 but broke down in tears before he could finish.

"THE DONG WITH THE LUMINOUS NOSE"

Lear wrote to his friend Fortescue on January 1, 1870, that he was working to "heap together all the nonsense I can for my new book which is entitled

Learical Lyrics
and Puffles of Prose,
&c. &c."

Certainly the Dong was a nonsense character, but there is the strong element of the "plaintive piper" in search of his Jumbly Girl that removes this verse from the element of nonsense. The falling meter and assonance of the words belie the title under which Lear's book was eventually published, *Laughable Lyrics: A Fourth Book of Nonsense, Poems, Songs, Botany, Music, &c.*

Readers may laugh at the picture of the Dong or the way in which he fashioned his "wondrous Nose" but his fruitless search through the night is not the stuff of nonsense. This is very much a "Learical Lyric" in the same genre as "The Courtship of the Yonghy-Bonghy-Bò" and "Incidents in the Life of My Uncle Arly."

"Incidents in the Life of My Uncle Arly"

In 1884 Lear sent the first stanza of this autobiographical poem to Fortescue, "just to let you know how your aged friend goes on." The last lines, changed in the published version, read:

> But his shoes were far too tight!
> Too! Too!
>   far too tight!

The verse, begun for Lady Evelyn Baring, was finished in 1885. Lear made copies and sent them to friends.

Lear's "First-class Railway-Ticket" was, of course, his introduction into English society. Unlike his society friends, Lear had "subsisted . . . by his own exertions," his art, just as Uncle Arly sold "Propter's Nicodemus Pills." Lear had seen the "Tiniskoop-hills" many times over, and wandered "three-and-forty winters" from 1827 when he left his childhood home, Bowman's Lodge, until 1870 when he settled at Villa Emily.

"The Pelican Chorus"

Lear began his career in art by drawing birds and remained devoted to them throughout his lifetime. On a trip through Greece in 1848 he "observed an infinite number of what appeared to be large white stones, arranged in rows with great regularity, though yet with something odd in their form not easily to be described. . . . I resolved to examine these mysterious white stones forthwith, and off we went, when—lo! on my near approach, one and all put forth legs, long necks, and great wings, and 'stood confessed' so many great pelicans, which, with croakings expressive of great disgust at all such ill-timed interruptions rose up into the air in a body of five or six hundred, and soared slowly away to the cliffs north of the gulf." Lear's guide, he records, "nearly fell off his horse with laughter at my surprise at the transmutation of the white stones." Certainly these are some of the birds who crept into this poem, published in *Laughable Lyrics* in 1877.

During his journey in Egypt in 1864, he saw birds by the hundreds who "stood in lines along the narrow sand-pits." In his diary he noted "4 black storks—one legged: apart—8 pelicans—careless, foolish. 17 small ducks, cohesive. 25 herons—watching variously posed: & 2 or 3 flocks of lovely ivory ibis."

Because Edward Lear could neither read nor write music, he hired Professor Pomé of San Remo to transcribe his music for piano.

"The Pobble Who Has No Toes"

"Thank the Lord that you are not a centipede!" Lear wrote to Lord Carlingford in December, 1883, "a burst of gratitude I feel every Sunday morning because on that day happens the weekly cutting of toenails and general arrangement of toes,—and if that is a bore with ten toes, what would it have been if it had been the will of Heaven to make up with a hundred feet, instead of only two—i.e. with five hundred toenails? It has been before now a subject of placid reflection and conjecture to me, as to whether Sovereigns, Princes, Dukes and even Peers generally—cut their own toenails. It is useless to think of asking hereditary Peery individuals about this as they are brought up to recognise facts as so to speak impersonal and beyond remark. . . ."

Lear wrote "The Pobble" just before his sixty-first birthday in 1873. It was published in *Laughable Lyrics* (1877).

"How Pleasant to Know Mr. Lear!"

Several of Lear's biographers mention that this verse was written by Lear and a girl, Miss Bevan, in April of 1879 in San Remo. Constance Strachey has suggested that Miss Bevan repeated to Lear a phrase she had overheard, "How pleasant to know Mr. Lear" and this formed the basis for the poem.

It would seem that this poem, with its careful quatrain pattern, crafted rhyme and meter, could hardly be the work of a young girl, nor would many of the phrases—"ill-tempered and queer," "concrete and fastidious," "his visage is more or less hideous"—be the work of a child.

The title, then, might certainly be the spark, as well as a phrase or two, but the verse itself must be the work of Lear.

Teapots and Quails

Published in England in 1953 and in America in 1954, this book contains material reproduced from drawings and manuscripts not published during Lear's lifetime. Much of it had been willed to Lear's friend, Sir Franklin Lushington, and another friend, Lord Northbrook.

Private collectors, most notably William B. Osgood Field and Philip Hofer, and others, placed their Lear material in the Harvard College Library which now houses the most extensive collection of "Leariana" in the United States.

This book includes five selections from *Teapots and Quails*: "Chimnies and Wings," "The Dish Tree," "Herons and Sweeps," "Puddings and beams," and "Wafers and Bears."

Index of Titles and First Lines